For Gemk,

Whose endless supply of ideas and honest critique made this possible.

感謝 Gemk

源源不絕的靈感及誠懇的建議讓這一切成真。

The Nodding Noodles

會點頭的麵條

Coleen Reddy 著

武建華・張維采 繪

薛慧儀 譯

三民書局

In a small village in China, something very strange happened one day.
A little boy named Lin Tee had just come home from school.
He was going to eat the same thing he ate every day—a bowl of noodles.

在中國的一個小村子裡，有天發生了一件非常奇怪的事情。
有個叫做林悌的小男孩剛從學校回到家裡，
打算吃一樣他每天都會吃的東西：一碗麵。

4

He sat down and was about to start eating his noodles.
"I wonder if it will rain today?" he said aloud to himself.
Then the most extraordinary thing happened.

他坐下來，正要開始吃麵時，
自言自語地說：「不知道今天會不會下雨呢？」
令人驚奇的事情就發生了。

As if the noodles heard his question, they nodded.
It was as though the noodles had answered his question.
Lin Tee screamed and went to get his mom.

麵條像是聽到了他的問話，居然點了點頭！
好像在回答他的問題一樣。
林悌大叫一聲，跑出去找他媽媽。

His mom was outside drinking tea.

"Mom, come quick! The noodles are nodding. I was wondering whether it would rain and the noodles nodded!" Lin Tee cried excitedly. Just then, they heard loud thunder and it started raining!

他的媽媽正在屋外喝茶。

「媽！快來！我的麵條在點頭耶！我剛剛在想會不會下雨，結果麵條就點頭了耶！」林悌興奮地喊著。

馬上，他們就聽見很大的打雷聲，果真開始下雨了！

9

"Let me see these noodles."
His mom looked at the noodles.
"They look like normal noodles," said his mom.

「讓我瞧瞧這些麵條。」
媽媽看了看麵條。
「它們看起來和一般的麵條沒什麼兩樣嘛！」他媽媽說。

Then she asked, "Noodles, does my husband hide his money?"
The noodles nodded up and down.
"Son, these are not normal noodles. These are special noodles.
They have the spirit of our ancestors. How else would they know
that your father hides his money?"

然後她問：「麵條呀！我老公有沒有藏私房錢呀？」
麵條上上下下地點起頭來。
「兒子呀！這可不是普通的麵條唷！它們是很特別的麵條，擁有
老祖先的靈魂，不然它們怎麼會知道你爸爸有藏私房錢呢？」

13

Pretty soon, the whole village had heard about the nodding noodles.
From all over, people came to ask them questions.
Lin Tee and his bowl of nodding noodles became quite famous.

很快地，整個村莊都知道了這碗會點頭的麵條。
來自各地的人們紛紛前來問麵條問題。
現在林悌和他那碗會點頭的麵變得遠近馳名了。

14

16

One day, the King himself came.

"Will my enemies attack me at night?" asked the King.

The noodles did nothing.

"Will the enemies attack me during the day?"

The noodles nodded up and down.

The king was happy.

He gave Lin Tee and his family lots of money.

有一天，國王親自來到村裡。

國王問：「我的敵人會不會在晚上攻擊我？」

麵條一動也不動。

「那麼敵人是在白天攻擊我嗎？」

麵條上上下下地點起頭來。

國王非常高興。

他給了林悌和他的家人很多錢。

All over the village, people looked at their bowls of noodles differently.
Instead of just eating the noodles, people would make sure that they
were just ordinary noodles and not nodding noodles.

現在全村莊的人都用不同的眼光看待自己碗中的麵條。
大家在吃麵前，都要先確定一下自己吃的只是普通的麵條，
而不是會點頭的麵條。

It started a new tradition. Before eating noodles, people would ask them a question to see if they nodded. Noodles became of special importance. The price of noodles went up and they became the most expensive food. Some families stopped eating noodles because they were too expensive and considered holy.

它開啟了一個新的習俗。

在吃麵前，大家都會先問麵條問題，看看麵條會不會點頭。

麵條變得具有特殊的重要性，而且被認為是神聖的束西。

麵條的價錢不停地上漲，變成最昂貴的食物。

有些家庭甚至不吃麵條了，因為實在太貴了！

But Lin Tee noticed something strange.
Every day, his noodles seemed to get shorter and shorter.
He was worried.
He didn't want his noodles to disappear.

但林悌注意到有件事情不太對勁。
他的麵條好像變得一天比一天短了。
他有點擔心。
他可不希望麵條消失呀！

So, he started adding fresh, new noodles to the bowl.
People would come to his house and ask the noodles questions.
But after they left, the new noodles would be shorter again.

所以，他開始在碗裡添加新的麵條。
大家仍然不斷地到他家裡來問麵條問題。
但只要他們一離開，新添進去的麵條又變短了！

24

25

It was clear that answering questions made the noodles shorter.
So, Lin Tee would have to add new noodles to the bowl every day.
He didn't mind. He was happy as long as the noodles kept nodding.

很明顯地，回答問題會讓麵條變短。
於是林悌每天都必須在碗裡加入新的麵條。
這他倒是不怎麼介意，只要麵條仍然會點頭，
他就很開心。

27

One day though, Lin Tee forgot to put new noodles in the bowl.
The next morning when he got up, he ran to his bowl of noodles.
He screamed when he saw what was in the bowl.

但是有一天，林悌忘了在碗裡加進新的麵條。
第二天早上他起床後，趕緊跑去看看他的那碗麵。
當他看到碗裡的東西時，不禁大叫了出來！

The noodles had completely disappeared.
The bowl was empty except for a big, fat NEWT.
"It wasn't the noodles. It was you, nodding under the
noodles all along, wasn't it?" Lin Tee asked the newt.
The newt grinned and nodded!
Then he wobbled off, out of the house,
to find another delicious bowl of noodles.

麵條全都不見了！
碗裡除了一隻大大的胖蠑螈外，什麼都沒有！
「原來不是麵條在點頭，是你呀！你一直都躲在
麵條底下點頭對不對？」林悌問這隻蠑螈。
蠑螈咧開嘴笑了起來，點了點頭。
然後牠搖晃著胖嘟嘟的身子爬出麵碗，離開屋子，
去找另一碗好吃的麵條囉！

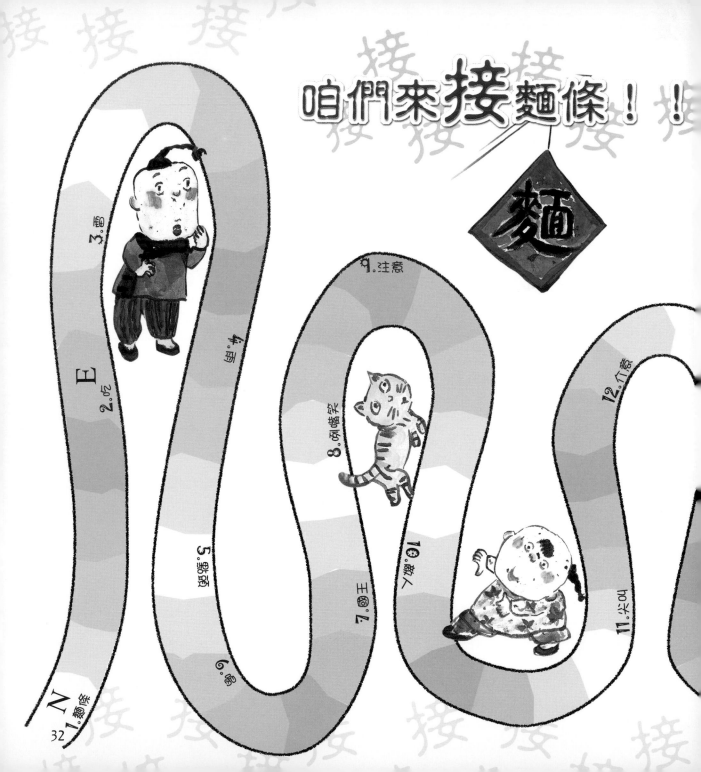

小朋友，你知道嗎？中國人一向深信過年時吃的麵條越長，自己的壽命就越長。現在就讓我們來玩個接麵條的遊戲。麵條上的數字就是題號，然後按下 track3，你會聽到林姊念出題號然後拼出「生字」，再將聽到的生字填在正確的位置（林姊念的時候，題號不會按照順序喔！）。

＊ 要特別注意喔，在麵條上，前一個生字的了尾跟後　個生字的字首共用同一格喔！

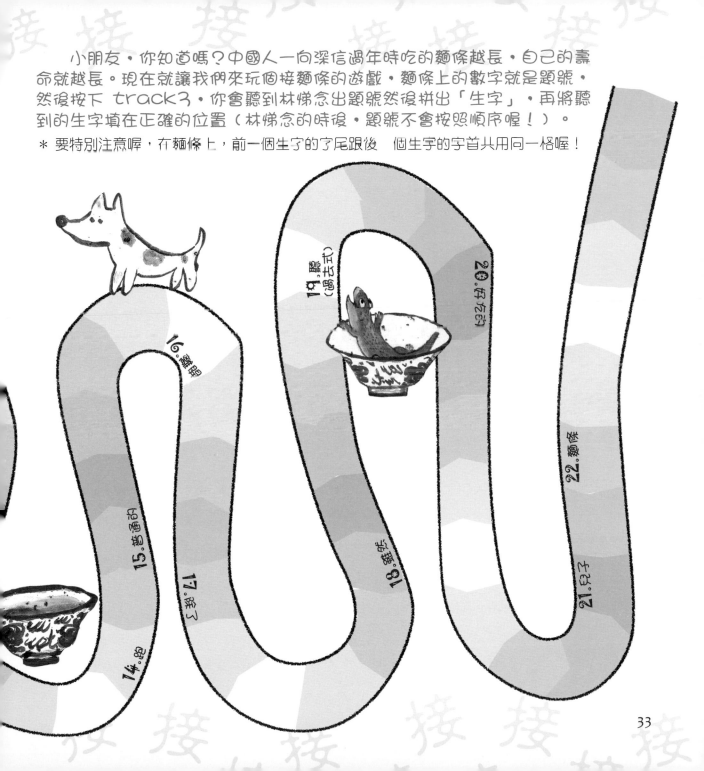

14. 跑
15. 普通的
16. 蟲卵
17. 跌了
18. 雖然
19. 聽（過去式）
20. 好吃的
21. 兒子
22. 麵條

生字表

全新創作 英文讀本
帶給你優格（yogurt）般，青春的酸甜滋味！

Teens' Chronicles

愛閱雙語叢書

青春記事簿

大維的驚奇派對／秀寶貝，說故事／杰生的大秘密
傑克的戀愛初體驗／誰是他爸爸？
叛逆大維打工記／外星老師來上課／耶！放假了！

你我身上純真的影子，
透過一篇篇幽默風趣的故事重現，
推薦你這套青春無悔的創作系列，
讓愛玫、杰生、大維、凱爾、海倫、傑克，
帶你進入他們的世界，品味另一種學習英語的全新感受。

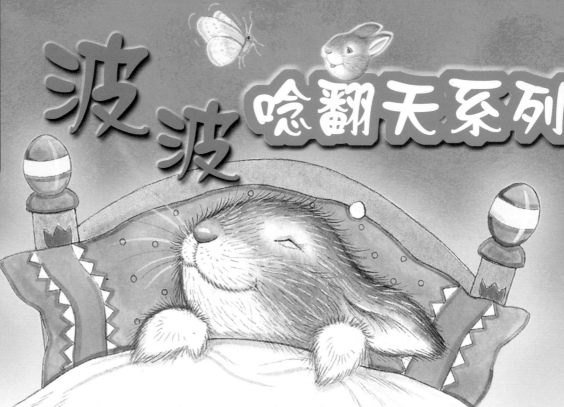

國家圖書館出版品預行編目資料

The Nodding Noodles:會點頭的麵條 / Coleen Red-
dy著; 武建華, 張維采繪; 薛慧儀譯. ──初版一
刷. ──臺北市；三民，2003
　　面； 公分──(愛閱雙語叢書.二十六個妙朋
友系列) 中英對照
　ISBN 957–14–3765–4 （精裝）

　1.英國語言－讀本

523.38　　　　　　　　　　　　　　92008804

© The Nodding Noodles
── 會點頭的麵條

著作人	Coleen Reddy
繪　圖	武建華　張維采
譯　者	薛慧儀
發行人	劉振強
著作財產權人	三民書局股份有限公司 臺北市復興北路386號
發行所	三民書局股份有限公司 地址／臺北市復興北路386號 電話／(02)25006600 郵撥／0009998–5
印刷所	三民書局股份有限公司
門市部	復北店／臺北市復興北路386號 重南店／臺北市重慶南路一段61號

初版一刷　2003年7月
編　號　S 85647–1
定　價　新臺幣壹佰捌拾元整
行政院新聞局登記證局版臺業字第○二○○號

ISBN　957–14–3765–4　（精裝）